This sketchBook Belong to :

Made in the USA
Monee, IL
22 April 2022

95211783R00063